I0456529

PREQUEL TO THE SHOCKWAVE SERIES

THE FALL

LAURA JUNTUNEN

THE FALL

PREQUEL TO
THE SHOCKWAVE SERIES

LAURA JUNTUNEN

Copyright © 2023 Laura Juntunen

All rights reserved, including the right to reproduce this book or portions thereof in any form whatsoever.

This is a work of fiction. Names, characters, places, and incidents either are the products of the author's imagination or are used fictitiously. Any resemblance to actual persons, living or dead, businesses, companies, events, or locales is entirely coincidental.

Paperback ISBN: 978-1-955010-17-7
eBook ISBN: 978-1-955010-16-0

Cover Design by Laura Juntunen

THE FALL

CHAPTER 1

A screen illuminated the far side of the conference room, taking up the entire wall. A dark office shown through the monitor. Bookshelves filled with untouched books lined the space around an empty desk. Someone clearly designed the space for aesthetics rather than use.

The audio connected. A shuffling sound preceded the man as he came into view: the Director. He jostled himself into the leather chair behind the desk. It creaked with his weight, straining as he moved. A small lamp clicked on and brightened the picture.

The Director continued to get himself comfortable on the screen. Gretchen did the same in the conference room. She sat in one of the twelve seats available to her, watching a secretary scurry about the side of the room. The young woman cleaned a puddle on the beverage station, having broken a bottle of water. The liquid streamed across the table and absorbed into a stack of napkins near the edge.

A cough from the TV interrupted the nearly silent room. Gretchen brought her attention back to the man. She repositioned herself, trying to ignore the pinch at the front of her left shoe. The Director sat square to the camera, his full attention on the conference call. He smirked and cleared his throat once more.

"Sir," Gretchen nodded in acknowledgment.

The Director wore a crisp white suit. It shone in the dim room, as if he and his power were glowing. Gretchen did not lose the irony of his clothing. Behind his back, he was called "The Shadow." This was for his habit of showing up unannounced and from the corners of empty rooms. She preferred to call him "The Whale." His colossal size and slow demeanor took charge in any room he occupied, even through a screen. The nickname was more to cut down the intimidation factor for Gretchen. Though it only worked half the time. No matter what she called him in her mind, he was still an insufferable person, tough to be around and work for.

"Gretchen," the Director said, nodding to her. His eyes flickered to the space behind her. "Excuse me, you in the back?"

The secretary, still cleaning the mess, looked up. She flushed scarlet and froze. Gretchen could nearly hear the secretary's heart hammering through her chest.

"Director, my apologies," the secretary whispered.

"Yes, well, can you please make your way from the conference room? I have important business to discuss with Ms. Weber here. That's a good girl." His eyes left the screen before he could see the young woman's reaction.

Gretchen watched as the secretary's face flushed yet again, alarmed to be acknowledged by the leader of their organization. She nodded, piling up the wet napkins on the table. She shuffled from the room and shut the door behind her.

Gretchen turned back to the screen. "Sir," she repeated, nodding once more. She knew perfectly well his pleasantries toward the secretary were a facade. She anchored herself in her seat, ready for his true colors to come barreling toward her.

The Director was fierce. Unapologetic. Cut-throat. He had worked his way through the company for the past thirty years, slowly gaining majority ownership by buying off small percentages at a time. Though he was supposed to report to the board and gain their approval on matters, he held control and wielded it to benefit himself. Gretchen braced herself for him to do exactly that, but he didn't speak. He sat, stirring papers around on his desk, contorting with thought as he read through files Gretchen was sure were about her project.

"Are you ready, Sir?" Gretchen spoke up once more.

He shifted from thought to irritation. A grim snarl met her gaze. "Do you think I would come to a meeting unprepared?" He didn't wait for her to answer as he cleared his throat. "Of course, I'm ready. You're the one who has a project up in flames, figuratively and literally. It's in your best interests to be ready."

His scratchy vocals led Gretchen to believe he'd been overusing his power in the last few hours. She recalled his tyrannical raids on the office. She felt relieved she didn't have to work in the same building as him anymore. The boss reached off screen and came back with a lit cigar between his thumb and finger. The smoke swirled up as he puffed the toxic air.

"Well, get on with it," he said.

"There was an outbreak," Gretchen started. "We lost fifteen test subjects, ages ranged from newborn to the eldest being twenty-three." She refused to break eye contact with the monitor. Though she didn't know the location of the camera, she knew the general place to look. She refused to look down, to look weak in front of this monster. "The outbreak is still undergoing investig…"

"I know about the outbreak, woman!" His voice slammed into her. "Last month, the project was a success. You gained ground, you found answers, and you were closer to an exact formula; a precautionary tool to protect against the device. Why isn't that intel on my desk?"

"Yes, that's true," Gretchen dropped her chin slightly. "I had a formula to prevent the negative effects of the energy. But once people started dying, we had to run further tests to confirm the formula wasn't what caused the outbreak."

"And?"

"The results were inconclusive. We couldn't come to

an agreement on if our tests caused the outbreak."

"Because your lab went up in flames, I suppose?" The man interrupted. His face reddened and grew hard. "How convenient. What new information can you tell me, Ms. Weber? Anything useful?"

Gretchen watched the cigar smoke waft around the man, floating out of view on the screen. She saw the smoke in her memory, heard the screams of the quarantined patients as they burned to death, trapped in the make-shift laboratory.

"All my records are gone," she shook her head. She still hadn't grasped the damage of the fire herself, the eradication of her entire career.

"Gone? Just like that," he snapped his fingers.

His whispered words tracked a chill up Gretchen's back. She nodded.

"And who started the fire?"

"I…I don't know." Her palms grew clammy. She tried to hide them under the table as she attempted to wipe them dry. "It wasn't me. Or my team. I can promise you that."

"And this has nothing to do with the outbreak? Or so you claim." His words trailed off.

"They were two isolated incidents." Gretchen's gaze shot to the man's, appalled he would insinuate a connection. "The outbreak was contained."

"I got a report on my desk regarding the outbreak. Now, here we are with a new report elaborating a completely different incident from that same lab. Yet you're refusing to believe the two incidents are related.

How can two attempts at destroying your work not be connected?"

Gretchen flinched. The outbreak hadn't been her fault, nor had anyone on her team been responsible, she was certain.

"The patients contracted a virus and began dropping like flies. It wasn't intentional. We were able to contain it to a small group of patients. All those infected were lost. With the outbreak under control, we went back in to continue our studies, to ensure the outbreak was not related to our work."

"You just said you never found evidence it wasn't correlated." The man stroked his chin. "So, it could be internal sabotage, yes?"

Gretchen ignored his interruption, knowing neither of them could assume an answer to his question. "Soon after the outbreak settled, the fire broke out. It took out the entire laboratory, three recovering patients, along with a few deceased subjects we were still studying."

"And the fire took all your work with it. Now, that sounds like sabotage," he repeated his thought. "You don't think the outbreak was vandalism to begin with? Once their first attempt failed, the vandal would need to come up with another way to stop the project. Yes? So, he put it up in smoke." The man puffed a round cloud from his mouth. "It seems to me you have a traitor on your team."

"No one on my team would have done this." Gretchen stood from her chair. Once an idea sparked, it was hard to change this man's mind. She thought of the files piled in her hotel safe. They were all that were saved from the fire, barely significant. She decided against telling the Director about them. These files wouldn't tell him anything about who set the fire, or if it was intentional. It could have been an accident. She groaned. She looked at all the clues, spoke to her team, and knew none of them would go against her.

"Sit down, woman," the Director growled.

Gretchen obliged, only because of the throbbing in her foot. It would only grow worse if she remained standing. She straightened her shirt and sat, looking back at the screen with an attempt at a calm demeanor.

"What about Mr. Friedman?" The Director flicked the end of his cigar into his ash tray. "He's seen success in every step of his journey. He's only been with the company for what? A year?" His eyebrow lifted. "You've been working on your little idea for twenty-five years and only just now found the formula to prevent negative reactions from the machine. Twenty-five years of work up in flames." He paused, relishing the control he held. "You're telling me you can't remember any of the formulas, any of the data to replicate it?"

"It's not that easy," she said. "And you know Friedman's project has nothing to do with this."

"It's not that easy, or are you hiding it?" He ignored the Friedman comment, as she knew he would, and pushed on. "Did you sabotage your own lab to hide something?"

Gretchen knew this would be an angle he would bring up. She knew he would suspect foul play.

"I've been working on this, like you said, for over

twenty-five years. Once my lab partner passed away, I continued on with our research."

"Well, it sounds like she was the brains of the operation. You took twenty-five years to catch up to where she was when she died," his interruption punched her in the stomach.

"I didn't *catch up* to her. We never reached this level of research when she was alive. And she didn't just die, she was murdered. Her and her husband. We all know it." As soon as the words left her lips, her heart sank to her stomach. It was one thing to conspire the truth with trusted colleagues, it was quite another to voice them aloud.

"Don't you dare talk about that family," the man's snarl crept out of the darkness. He had leaned back nearly out of frame since starting their conversation, but now his face came into full light. The lines wrapping around his eyes deepened. She could almost see remorse in his gaze, but then he moved back into the shadows.

Gretchen took a breath, the weight of his unsaid threat lingering around her. She pushed on, "we created a formula and now it's destroyed. Regardless of if the laboratory fire was sabotage, as you suggested, the formula is still gone. We can't replicate it without my notes. I can only start from scratch at this point."

"There's no time to start from scratch," he huffed. "This project was supposed to be complete by now."

"This project will never be complete," Gretchen squeezed her eyes shut in frustration. "They promised me 20 more years with those babies…"

"You've worked with some subjects for 25 years. What difference would another newborn test subject make?" The man slammed his fist onto the desk, sloshing the brown liquid in an elaborate whiskey decanter positioned toward the edge of the screen.

Gretchen watched the liquid dance. The man's face went from beet red to a lighter pink as a long silence stretched between them. The liquid slowed to a light wave. The toes in her left shoe had grown numb. She wished she could take them off to release the pressure. She was grateful for the distraction, no matter how painful.

Finally, the man took a breath. "You've gathered all your things from the facility, yes?"

Gretchen nodded. "I have my plane ticket to meet at headquarters tomorrow."

"No, we need you here sooner than that," he picked up the phone on his desk and punched it with his sausage fingers. "You have a lot of explaining to do, Ms. Weber. My secretary will put you on this morning's flight. If you're going to make it, you better start running."

The monitor went black.

THE FALL

CHAPTER 2

G retchen sprinted from the room, her suffocated toes now causing pins and needles to shoot into her ankle. She turned toward the front entrance, pulling her jacket on as she went.

How dare he bring Friedman into the conversation? She knew her colleague's success was setting him apart from her, leading him to an approaching promotion and company advancement. As the thought drifted through her mind, she saw Friedman sprinting across the lobby. She scoffed, knowing the Director had given them the same orders. She hoped their seats would not be near one another on the plane. Friedman would have questions about the fire.

Knowing she would barely have time to grab her things from the hotel, Gretchen contemplated leaving them behind. Everything was replaceable. Trying to hail a nearby cab, she remembered her files.

The only files that survived the fire in her laboratory were sitting in her hotel room safe. She would need to retrieve them. Waving an apology to the cabbie who stopped for her, she crossed the busy intersection on foot. The hotel was only a few blocks away. She could make it there fastest by walking, despite her aching toes begging her to reconsider.

Gretchen weaved her way through the crowd, quickly approaching her hotel. She pulled her phone from her pocket and dialed the concierge desk.

"Maple Plaz…"

"Gary?" She cut off the gruff voice that answered. "It's Gretchen, from 504. Can you call me a quick-blitz cab?"

"Yes, ma'am." His voice was firm and kind, just like his presence. "Is everything all right?"

Gretchen could hear him scribble a note on paper. Always the rule follower, Gary logged and tracked every request to completion.

"Yes, thank you." She sprinted down the last few steps of the sidewalk and pulled the front door of the hotel open. She could see Gary across the lobby and waved.

"Where did you-" A puzzled look came across his face. He had torn his gaze from the mob of tourists lined up to speak to him to see who entered the lobby. Seeing Gretchen's wave, he shook his head.

"No time to explain," Gretchen spoke into the phone as she caught his smirk. "I've learned quick, huh?" She smiled.

Her first attempt to speak to the concierge did not go smoothly. She had to wait in line for over twenty minutes as the non-locals asked for directions and recommendations. Why they didn't do a Google search was beyond her, but she stood and waited patiently. During those twenty minutes, Gretchen watched the concierge and noticed, with quiet amusement, that every time the phone rang, the person on the line was given preference to the person standing in the lobby. Sometimes using tech in a once tech-less world proved valuable.

"You've sure learned quick. Look at you! And speaking of the way you look; you seem to be in quite a rush. I'll be sure to tell the cabbie there's a fat tip waiting if they get here quick." Gary chuckled into the phone as he smiled over the mob of tourists.

"Gary, you're the best!" Gretchen made it to the elevator, having to weave around the tourists, all eager to speak to her friend. "I'll be down in five minutes."

Scrambling through her hotel room, she pulled her belongings together. She set her packed bag by the door and turned to the nightstand between the two queen-sized beds. Squatting down, she plugged in her code for the hotel room safe. The door popped open and revealed her files.

As she stood, files in hand, a sharp rap knocked on the door, breaking the silence in the space. She sucked in a breath and made her way to the door, yanking it open.

"Vic?" A middle-aged man with graying hair stood before her. She had left him in the facility, he being one personnel allowed to remain on site after the fire. Vic was her friend, a confidant and ally. Why he stood at the threshold of her hotel room and not in the facility where he belonged, she wasn't sure. "What are you doing here?"

"Hello, my dear," the man smiled, his sly grin that of a man on a mission. "What a welcome, but I know you're in a rush. Let's get a move on." He motioned toward the elevators.

"Vic," Gretchen repeated, grabbing her belongings scattered across the room. "Sorry, I'm just surprised to see you. Why are you here?"

"I'm trying to convince you to stay," he shrugged, watching her bundle the rest of her belongings together. Once ready, he led her to the elevators. A briefcase jarred the door open. Once the pair entered, Vic pulled the case from the opening and the door slid shut.

"Clever," Gretchen smirked, knowing Vic always had a plan in place. She wiped her brow, a fierce sweat now seeping down the back of her shirt. "I'm on the way to the airport. I can't even think about staying here." She eyed her friend wearily, challenging his knowledge. "How did you know I was in a hurry?"

"Oh, my dear," Vic chuckled. "I am always in the know."

"So, you knew I was going to the airport?"

"Of course. But I want you to start your research from scratch." He crossed his arms. "You and I both know your work here is more important than in Vegas."

"How do you know where I'm going?" Gretchen

asked, knowing Vic had sources he would never reveal. She shook her head. She should have learned by now. Vic would always know more about her role in the company than she ever would.

"Don't act childish. Of course, I know where you're going," Vic said. "You're being sucked in by the Director, getting pulled back to the base to give him more intel. Am I wrong?"

The elevator jolted to a stop on the second floor and a family of four entered. They forced Gretchen and Vic into the corners. They shared a glance, knowing they couldn't continue their conversation with anyone in earshot. The elevator closed, resumed its descent, and quickly opened on the first floor. The family ambled out, filled with laughter and chatter. Gretchen sped past them.

"Gary, is the car here?" Gretchen yelled across the lobby to catch the concierge's attention. She caught the attention of some tourists as well. They eyed her with irritation. Gary nodded and waved a hand toward a black car outside the front doors. "Thanks! I'll stop by next time I'm in town," she locked eyes with Gray, scowling and rolling her eyes toward the tourists. Gary caught her message and shrugged. It was just another day in his life as a concierge.

Gretchen pushed open the front door, her bag and laptop case flinging around wildly. Vic was close on her heels, trying to help but failing miserably. She slipped into the black car, making room for Vic to join her. Once settled, she pushed the partition button, closing off the front of the car from its rear. With the soundproof enclosure between them and the driver, she turned to Vic.

"You know I can't continue research without approval from the top," she sighed. "I can't stay. I need to go to Vegas and plead my case to the board. With the right funding, I'll be back within the month."

Vic hesitated, refusing to say a word as Gretchen stared at him.

"What, no rebuttal?"

"You know I don't always follow protocol, and I think this would be the perfect time to skip asking for permission and push forward. You can ask for forgiveness when they're handing you a Nobel Prize," Vic shrugged. "And who knows, they might not even notice you missing. They won't know you're working with me unless someone tells them. They'll assume you've quit."

"No, not a chance, and you're too smart to suggest that," Gretchen whispered. "The Director thinks someone from the inside sabotaged my experiments. From the sound of it, he won't forget about this. He's adamant about getting answers. If I *disappear*, he'd have scouts out by nightfall."

Vic nodded. Though Gretchen could tell he didn't agree with all she was saying, he was simply allowing her to vent. He was good at listening, even if it took up precious time.

"I need funding, Vic," she sighed. "I need new equipment. Everything went up in smoke. And I need lab techs. My team has all dispersed across the country.

There's no way I can call them back. Especially if I can't promise any type of salary for their research."

Vic nodded. "But you're considering it, then?"

Gretchen rolled her eyes. "You know I can't consider staying against orders." She pushed her laptop bag from her feet as the cab sped around a corner. For being a premium cab service, there was little room in the back seat.

"What if we taught the civilians?"

"What do you mean? Teach them the lab work? Are you insane?" Gretchen scoffed at the idea. "You know the patients and civilians are tense about what happened. You can't expect them to play along. Some of them have family in the trials, some even lost loved ones in the outbreak. They'd never help me."

Vic shrugged again, irritating Gretchen further.

"The answer is no, Vic," she pushed her eyes with the palms of her hands. A migraine was setting in. "I need to follow orders and get to Vegas. I need to talk to the board and get funding. Unless you have a few million lying around that no one knows about?"

"Wouldn't you like to know?"

A long pause settled the tension in the vehicle. The sound of the freeway buzzed in the background as they sped through the city.

"Please don't get on that plane," Vic turned to Gretchen.

The woman hesitated. She knew that tone. That was the sound of worry and secrecy. "What aren't you telling me, Vic?"

The man turned away, looking out the window. The silence enveloped them as they neared the airport.

"Vic?" Gretchen probed further, pulling his shoulder toward her so he had to look at her.

"I'm not withholding anything," he said, rolling his eyes.

"Yes, you are." Gretchen pointed a finger at her friend. She knew his eye roll was for show. He was worried.

"Just…" his voice faltered. "Gretch, don't get on that plane."

The partition lowered. The driver came into view and his eyes locked onto Gretchen's in the rear-view mirror. "We're here, Ma'am," the driver put the car in park and pushed his door open.

The airport departures entrance was staring Gretchen down. The driver pulled open her door, holding his hand out to support her from the vehicle. She ignored him and turned back to her friend.

"What's going on, Vic?" She pleaded with him. "This isn't like you. Something's going on. You need to tell me now!"

Vic's eyes tightened. They had mere seconds.

"Vic!" Gretchen grabbed his shoulders. "I have to get on this plane. Tell me what's going on!"

"Ma'am?" The driver leaned down to peer into the vehicle.

Vic leaned over Gretchen and raised a single finger to the driver. He pulled the door shut. Now Gretchen knew he meant business. Her face reddened at the seriousness of the situation. She waited for him to speak.

"Before you board that plane," Vic whispered, "read the most recent updates on the drive."

"What? What updates?"

"You'll know which ones."

THE FALL

CHAPTER 3

T he airport security let Gretchen through quickly. The company she worked for wasn't directly linked to the government, but they had special clearance at all major airports and restricted areas. Gretchen had mid-level clearance, not as high as some, but she could get through the airport fairly quickly.

She rushed to her gate with her belongings and laptop in hand. The plane was still boarding. She had time to spare. While catching her breath, she walked to the end of the line to wait. She pulled her phone from her pocket. *What file is Vic talking about?* He said she'd know, but now she was second guessing herself.

Pulling up her secure wi-fi hotspot, she opened the shared company files. Her first instinct was to look into her own experiment files. The shared cloud held only partial documents. They kept most of the true research at the lab to avoid leaking to the public. She stepped forward a few paces, catching up to the person in front of her. The first passengers in line had entered the loading bridge to the airplane, and a steady stream followed their lead.

Nothing stood out in her experiment files and there were no files added within the last twenty-four hours. She searched through Friedman's shared documents. The sight of his name made her blood boil. They were colleagues and friends, yet the Director used his progress against her. She knew she couldn't hold it against Friedman. His work wasn't linked to her blood trials. They simply sought the same outcome: protection against the machine.

She glanced up, scanning the faces for the familiar smirk of her colleague. Friedman would be on this flight, but she couldn't see him among the crowd.

Sifting through the rest of Friedman's public files, she found nothing. Like her own files, they kept the majority offline. Two more paces forward. She was gaining ground and would board within minutes.

What do you want me to find, Vic?

She froze. *Recent update.* Vic didn't simply say to view any shared files. He specifically said to view the recent updates. *The updates record.* On the first page of the shared drive, there was a list of files which circulated. The list tracked updates. All she'd have to do was change the viewing to 'most recently updated.' She cursed under her breath, wondering why she hadn't thought of it sooner.

"Clumsy mistake," she mumbled, looking at files at the

top of the folder.

Caroline. Gretchen stared at the name of her colleague, the same woman who passed away twenty-five years earlier. There were no changes to the files since then. Now they were coming up, not only in the shared documents, but in her personal conversation with the Director. *What are the odds?*

She opened the file and read.

"Ma'am?" The gate attendant waved at Gretchen, motioning for her to step forward.

"I'm sorry," Gretchen smiled. "I didn't notice…" her voice trailed off as she flipped her phone to the airline app and pulled up her boarding pass. She placed it on the scanner and the beep admitted her to the long hallway of the plane. As she walked down the slope, she pulled up the files once more.

As she read, her heart rate soared. "The prick knew I was close," she cursed the Director. "That fat, pompous ass."

"Sounds like you could use a drink," a man behind her laughed. "Was it a co-worker or boss? Or husband?"

"Neither. Err, no." She clicked her phone screen off, hoping the man hadn't seen the words that still shook her to her core. She looked up and smiled. The balding man seemed kind enough. "It was just someone who's been hiding something, but it's all out in the open now. And I'm on my way to his office, so I'll be sure he gets what's coming to him."

The man's brows rose, oddly bushy for someone with

nearly no hair on the top of his head. "I'm glad I'm not that guy," he said.

Gretchen smiled at him, then winced as the feeling came back to her left toes. She leaned on the side of the terminal walk and pulled her shoe from her foot.

"So, it is time for a drink?" Her new acquaintance laughed as he pointed to her shoe.

"You have no idea," Gretchen laughed.

As she stepped onto the plane, she heard the faint whispers of the loudspeaker in the airport terminal: "Would a Mr. Friedman please make their way to gate seventeen? An Alec Friedman?"

CHAPTER 4

T he ding of the loudspeaker rang through the airport. "Friedman, an Alec Friedman, please report to terminal seventeen. Your flight has boarded. Five minutes to departure."

The loudspeaker blared overhead as a man sprinted down the busy hallway, dodging families and airport carts as he went. He winced as a bead of sweat seeped from his brow, plummeting into his eye. He pivoted around a couple who took an abrupt turn near a restaurant entrance. The movement flung his suitcase around, hitting a businesswoman on the back.

"Hey!" the woman yelled, pulling a slim phone from her ear. "Watch it!" She shook her phone at the man as he kept running, hardly turning to mumble an apology to the disheveled patrons he left behind.

I can't miss this bloody flight! The man stumbled over a package sitting next to a row of seats. "Are you kidding me?!"

"Mr. Friedman," the loudspeaker broke his irritation and turned it to worry. "Mr. Alec Friedman, last call for the flight to Las Vegas."

As the woman spoke the last word, the man threw himself at the entrance of his gate.

"I'm here!" Alec yelled, waving his hands back and forth. "I'm here! Wait!" Alec could see the gate attendant roll her eyes in frustration. He cursed her under his breath. As he jogged the rest of the way to the counter, he straightened his composure. "Alec Friedman, reporting for duty!" He plastered on a charming grin as he looked into the attendant's eyes.

The woman blushed and motioned for him to lower his phone screen to the scanner. A green light illuminated, and the machine beeped. The attendant ushered Alec down the jetway to board the plane.

The passengers cheered and shouted. Their applause displayed a communal appreciation for the latecomer. Alec waved his apologies as the collective mumbles settled.

"About time, man." The woman in the front row whispered under her breath. Alec noted her shoes already flung off, ready to settle in for the flight. The bald man next to her rolled his eyes, gesturing toward Alec with an air of superiority.

Alec ignored the man. "Hey, Gretch," he smirked at her, knowing she'd get over his tardiness soon.

The plane was full. Alec sunk into the row behind his colleague, seeing her roll her eyes. He chuckled to himself and watched as she asked the flight attendant for a drink and leaned herself back into her seat. She seemed tired, more than usual anyway. The short flight would be enough time for a quick doze, but Alec doubted he'd be able to sleep with everything on his mind.

Leaning between the seats in front of him, Alec uttered his apology, "Sorry, Gretch. I ran as fast as I could." He chuckled, hoping to get back onto her good side. The bald man eyed him, his face growing red.

"Right," Gretchen mumbled back. "And what would I have said to the Director if you missed the flight?" She immersed herself in her phone, reading files of some sort. Alec couldn't make out the words, but lines of text scrolled up under her thumb as she grazed the document.

"Aww, come on, Gretch," Alec put on his best flirting tone, his accent coming out thick. "You would never have let them fly off without me, and you know it." He sat back in his seat, lifting the window shade to look out onto the tarmac. "Plus, it wouldn't have been your fault if I missed the flight. The Director couldn't blame you for it."

Gretchen didn't acknowledge his words. She smiled at the flight attendant, who handed her a glass and a can of soda. A clear, round rock of ice sat at the bottom of the glass, clinking with every movement. "Thank you," she said. Alec could see her hand shake slightly as she held the glass on her knee and poured the soda.

The flight attendant moved to Alec's row, nodding her

chin to him. "Nothing for me, thanks," he said.

Gretchen turned around. "Think again," she whispered. "You'll need a drink to settle the shock of what I need to tell you." She motioned to her phone, still lit up and displaying the stream of words like before.

The balding man next to Gretchen grimaced and eyed Alec. She gave the man a small smile, but Alec could see Gretchen's irritation. Seeing it could be an issue, Alec engaged. "Do you mind?" Alec asked the stranger.

"Actually, I was going to ask if you two were going to be chatting through the seats all flight long," the man huffed, confirming Alec's prediction. There was a beat of heated silence. "I'll trade places with you."

Alec's demeanor shifted.

"Oh," Gretchen choked on her soda, obviously struck by surprise. Alec knew she wouldn't want to sit next to him, but he'd rather that than have to lean forward to converse for the entire flight.

"Actually, that'd be terrific, thank you!" Alec waved the man to switch spots with him.

Playing merry-go-round was distracting for the flight attendants, still finishing up their safety procedure.

"Excuse me," an attendant came up to the trio. "You all need to sit down." She squeezed past to help a passenger who had lit up their call button. "You must take your seats," she hissed at them. The tangle of bodies made for a curious sight. A murmur of comments came from around their seats.

"Sorry, sorry," the stranger smiled at the attendant.

"These two just said they'd buy my drinks for the flight if I swapped places with this guy here." He motioned to Gretchen and Alec.

Alec caught Gretchen's look of shock and smirked at her. "That's right," he turned to the flight attendant. "Get him whatever his little heart desires."

THE FALL

CHAPTER 5

The airplane hummed around the passengers, vibrating the seats and luggage in the overhead compartments. They had yet to leave their position on the tarmac.

"See," Alec leaned over to Gretchen. "I had plenty of time to get on the plane." He huffed in exhaustion, still getting settled into his new spot next to her. "And why did I need a drink?" He poured the amber liquid from the miniature bottle into the glass the flight attendant handed him. The round globe of ice bobbed as the whiskey embraced it. He eyed it with disgust, knowing his head would throb once they landed in Vegas. The moment of self-loathing drifted away as he took the first sip.

Silence lingered. Gretchen had just relayed her conversation with the Director to Alec. It turned out, he had a similar meeting with their boss. He didn't flinch at the mention of someone inside potentially being the culprit behind her experiment's destruction and the fire. Their boss said the same to him. In their conversation, the Director had also suggested Gretchen had something to do with the fire. He even asked Alec to question her about it on the flight. Alec kept that part of his meeting from Gretchen, knowing it wouldn't help their situation now.

Alec thought back to the moment the leadership forced him to leave the facility. The enclosure he created housed an entire population through renewable resources. After the fire, nearly all unessential employees were pushed out for safety reasons. The civilians who called the place their home could stay, which included all the test subjects from the trials. Gretchen and Alec were fast-tracked to the nearest city to stay in a hotel until given further orders. Since then, Alec hadn't seen her.

"Take another sip," Gretchen finally whispered to Alec, breaking him from his memories. "You'll need it. I have something to tell you." She paused as she took a sip of her soda. "Well, to show you, I guess. I wish this plane would just get in the air already."

"This delay won't last long." Alec's stomach clenched as the brown liquid coated his stomach.

"I've told you about Caroline, right?" Gretchen breached the subject.

Alec held his breath as the whiskey stung his insides. "Yeah, your first project partner," Alec shrugged. "What of her?"

"Someone updated one of our files this morning. It was regarding the machine. I think they added to the document to warn me…" she trailed off as the plane rolled forward. She passed him her phone.

Alec took the device from her and pressed his thumb to the screen, brightening it. He scrolled for a moment to see the length of the file; it was pages long. He glanced at her and she rolled her eyes, letting out a deep sigh. He smirked and scrolled back up to the top.

The file was from twenty years prior. He scanned the title, "Blood Trials 1: The Effects of EMP."

The first trial.

He scanned the file, looking for words that stood out. Then, without warning, a paragraph shone through. The font was slightly off, though it wouldn't be noticed by most. He had an eye for things like this. Gretchen shifted in her seat, seeing he'd spotted the information correctly.

Alec tried to make sense of the words. He understood the science behind them, but it was out of context and the details included his project, his electric dome. There was a date and time: today, mere hours from now. The file was twenty years old. Someone obviously tampered with it in order to send this message to Gretchen.

"Wait, what does this mean? Who sent this to you?"

"The machine is going to be tested," she ignored his second question.

"They wouldn't move forward without us. They need me in the room to pull up the protection protocols." Alec's mind swam with the idea, with the mayhem he would have to endure if they did not reach Las Vegas before the trial launched.

"Are you kidding?" Gretchen turned to face Alec. "They don't need you. Yes, you developed the force field technology, but you had an entire team of people helping. They all know how to run the program." She flipped her hair behind her shoulder. "I'm more worried about civilians getting caught in the crossfire. The Director knew I was close to blocking the pulse through our blood."

Alec could barely make out the last words, her voice growing quiet, contemplative. "Where are they pinpointing the pulse to land?" Alec asked, glancing back at the phone.

"It doesn't say."

Minutes ticked by. Alec continued to look at the files, his mind busy, no longer reading, but calculating. He glanced at his watch with irritation and worry. The plane moved further from the gate and made its way to the line of aircraft waiting to depart. Alec tried to do math in his head, contemplating their location and the time it would take to arrive in Las Vegas.

"Gretch," Alec leaned toward her. "If this timeline is right, we won't make it to Vegas before they begin."

"It'll launch in about two hours," Gretchen sighed deeply. "That's why Vic wanted me to stay behind."

"Vic? When did you talk to Vic?" Alec recalled the mousey Elder who helped lead the facility, always giving off an odd vibe. Despite this, Alec still trusted him without question or thought. He pulled Gretchen's shoulder, urging her to look at him. She refused. "Tell me when you spoke with Vic."

"We're going to make it. If the plane takes off in the next ten minutes, we'll be at the airport when the machine launches. We can contact the office for a pickup, but I think it'd be better to get a hold of someone personal. The Director wanted us in the air during this experiment. This delay isn't by chance." Her words were mumbles, thoughts being spoken aloud. Clearly she was ignoring Alec.

She pulled her phone from Alec's hand. He watched her fingers dance across the screen, navigating through emails and text messages faster than he could comprehend.

"We need to get off the plane," Alec whispered.

Gretchen's hands paused. She shot her gaze to his. "No way," she shook her head. "The test is launching from Vegas. If you want to be a part of it, we need to get there asap."

"What if we don't make it?" Alec sat up in his seat and felt a bead of sweat trickle down his back. He pulled his phone from his jacket pocket and scrolled through his contacts. He shot off a text, praying his prediction was wrong. "If Vic said to stay, you should have stayed."

"Stop. Vic was overreacting. We'll get there with time to evaluate the aftershocks," Gretchen hissed. "Or are you just so worried about your little bubble project?"

Alec could sense her tone, her jealousy. "Hey, don't be like that. Just because my experiments succeeded when yours imploded doesn't mean you can be a bitch about it."

Gretchen's face reddened, his words striking her with

force.

"It didn't *implode*. There has to be an explanation. My idea is more realistic to save human life. Your tool only saves the wealthy. I want to help everyone. You want to limit who gets protection."

"The *bubble*, as you call it, won't just protect the wealthy." Alec's thumb tapped on the armrest between them, unable to control itself. "I've just confirmed the wide expansion of its abilities. It can reach across the entire country now."

"There's no way." Gretchen turned to him. "You only just succeeded in protecting the community."

"And if it weren't for your little fire forcing us to pause our experiment, we would've been able to complete the next trial run before this…"

"That's why you want to get off the plane?"

"Partly. I wasn't thinking about my protection, if that's what you think." He rolled his eyes, his jaw clenching with irritation. "Vic said to stay, that's reason enough. It wouldn't surprise me if they test the limits of the machine against the force field. But it's finicky. I should be there to make sure all the numbers line up."

The pair grew silent. The soft buzz of passenger conversations surrounded them. No words were distinguishable against the mob of noise. The lights dimmed in the cabin.

"What can we do now? They won't let us jump from this thing on the runway." Gretchen locked eyes with Alec. There was a pause, an air of confusion about what to do next.

"Excuse me," a voice came over the plane's sound system. "Pardon for the interruption. We are next to depart." The pilot's voice was strained and dragged through the recycled air of the cabin. A chorus of sighs and exhaustion echoed his words.

The distraction came at the right moment, killing the electric energy circling around the colleagues. They both leaned into their seats, still reeling with thought, but too spent to voice their opinions further. The plane began its turn to the runway and the lights in the cabin dimmed further.

The plane lurched forward, pinning them to their seats.

Alec pulled his phone from his pocket, feeling the vibration of a text. He unlocked the screen as he felt the plane lift from the ground.

The wheels of the plane rumbled into their compartments. The sound of the doors closing banged from beneath, giving finality to their situation.

The text on Alec's screen drained the blood from his face.

Get off the plane!

THE FALL

CHAPTER 6

P anic ensued as the plane rose into the air, the pressure keeping Alec pinned to his seat. There was no way to get off the plane now. Sweat dripped from his forehead as he re-read the text, making sure he had read it correctly.

Get off the plane!

Indecision flew through him, unable to decide if he should text back or tell Gretchen what he just read. Both objectives were equally important, but he could not move forward with either. Fear enveloped him. He felt his breathing speed up. His shirt stuck to his skin. Droplets of sweat slid down his cheek.

The ding of the sound system jolted him. The plane

leveled out, removing pressure from his chest.

"Our snack and beverage service will pass through the cabin momentarily." The flight attendant announced. "There is slight turbulence. Please remain seated with your seat belts fastened. Thank you!"

Alec lost himself in thought, going over all the calculations from the past week. He had run the tests, on a small-scale of course, and everything ran smoothly. But he had a deep feeling of dread, of uncertainty. *What if something was off?* He questioned himself. Even one decimal point could make this project backfire. One person could sabotage the entire nation, just like Gretchen's experiments.

The realization dawned on him. Someone had tampered with Gretchen's project. And if there had been a traitor in the facility, it only made sense they were still inside, ready to do more damage. The fight to keep the project a secret was an ongoing concern, but if this was true, they had failed.

Alec was not in the security department, but his friend, the person who just texted him, was. She had been worried about the facility since the fire. She felt there were too many loose ends in the organization. Multiple entities worked on the project in many locations. They included Las Vegas, Seattle, D.C., and the facility itself, not to mention the overseas venues.

"Too many factors," Alec whispered to himself. There was no knowing where the traitor came from.

"Are you alright?" Gretchen put her hand on Alec's

arm. Her smirk was of reassurance, but she could not know what was truly going on in his mind. He had to tell her.

Finally, Alec took a deep breath and unlocked his phone screen once more. He typed.

Is it the machine?
We're in the air. I can't get off.

"Gretch," Alec nudged her and angled his phone toward her. She glanced down and paled.

"*Get off the plane?*" she whispered. "Who's that from?"

The phone buzzed in his hand. Another response.

Oscillation. They've taken over the machine.
We don't have control anymore.

Gretchen's eyes widened as she looked from the screen and up to Alec.

We've lost control. How could this happen?

The worry in his gut was now explained. He felt there was a security breach when the fire broke out in Gretchen's lab, but there was no sign of forced entry. The community leaders had done an investigation, and they deemed the incident isolated. But now they had confirmation, though it was too late. The facility was no longer an asset; it was a threat.

"Alec, who sent that message to you?"

He couldn't answer, he couldn't comprehend the

question, nor could he speak.

"Sir, would you like some water?" The flight attendant tapped his shoulder.

Alec shook his head. "No, I'll take liquor."

The attendant returned in record time and handed Alec the four small bottles he requested. All the while, Gretchen eyed him suspiciously. He assumed she would refuse if he offered, but he pushed two of the bottles toward her, regardless. She hesitated and after he urged her, she complied, wrapping her fingers around the tiny bottlenecks. He twisted the top off one of his bottles.

"Since we might die, be tipsy for it." The whisper was not audible to their neighboring passengers. There was no reason to cause an alarm. The fear in Gretchen's eyes was enough for Alec. He suddenly felt a wave of relief. He wasn't alone.

"You're jumping to conclusions." Gretchen glanced around the cabin, clutching the small bottles of whiskey. "Whoever took over the machine, they won't attack. Plus, we don't even know where they'd attack, if that's even the reason for taking over. Who was that text from?"

"A friend. She's in security. She takes care of routine business. Not really *routine* anymore." Alec tilted his head back and downed the first miniature bottle of liquor. "I don't want to be sober if it hits. Especially if we're in the air. If someone took over the machine, we're in deep water. Well, I suppose I should say we're in a free-fall," Alec smirked at his joke.

Gretchen's face told him it wasn't funny.

"Let's assume the worst," Alec sighed. "They have the power to strike anywhere in the country if they know how to pinpoint the impact. And even with my machine being able to protect the entire country, it's not an easy feat. If they had planned on testing my force-field, there's no chance they'll get the numbers right. They'd assume country-wide protection, and they'd get nation-wide destruction."

Gretchen flicked her eyes from Alec to the whiskey in her hand. She placed one in her lap and twisted off the cap of the other. She stared at the bottle. Alec could see her calculating her decision. He remembered the story of the last time she drank alcohol, nearly ten years before. The bender she went on had caused an accident, a death, and a divorce. Her sobriety was all she had left, and he knew that. But he had a feeling there was not much time left for either of them.

Alec twisted off the cap of his second bottle and raised it to the air in front of Gretchen. "To science," he said. "And the unknown world we may never see."

Gretchen winced, but raised her bottle to his and tapped their rims together. "To science," she repeated. Throwing her head back, Alec could see the small scar on her neck from the accident a decade before.

"To science," he whispered a second time. He poured the drink into his throat.

THE FALL

CHAPTER 7

A lec moaned, feeling his mind wander with drunkenness. "What was the purpose of your study?" His voice slurred from the alcohol taking root in his system.

Gretchen looked at him, her eyes not as blurred or shaky as his. He pondered how much alcohol it would take to get her drunk.

"What do you mean, what's the purpose?" Gretchen shook her head.

"I mean, do you really think you can cure civilians? Well, not cure, but prevent them from having effects from the pulses?" Alec asked, trying to drink from an empty whiskey bottle.

Gretchen studied her fingers. She hadn't said much since taking her first sip of alcohol. Alec wondered if she regretted the decision to break her sobriety. Before he could ask, she turned to him.

"I started working on the trials with Caroline," she began. "We had an understanding. We both thought the machine was dangerous. But we didn't have the power to stop the idea from becoming a reality. We were against it, along with many other people in the company, but we couldn't voice our concerns."

Alec nodded, remembering the rumors he'd heard when first being hired on to work for the company.

"If we spoke our mind, it'd mean disappearing under extreme and questionable circumstances." Gretchen pulled Alec back to the present. "Our blood trials, in theory, were going to change the molecular structure of the blood so the electric pulses couldn't affect the body in such a severe way. Keep in mind, the original machine obliterated people from the inside out. It was too strong. Over the last 20 years, they've been trying to modify it so we can protect people from being killed."

Gretchen paused, swirling the whiskey in her glass. After her first sip, straight from the bottle, she requested a glass of ice to water it down. Killing the sting of the alcohol wasn't something Alec wanted; he enjoyed the burn in his throat.

The ice was long gone. The watered-down whiskey hardly covered the full bottom of Gretchen's glass. Alec watched the amber tilt from one side of her glass to the other, wishing she would hand it to him.

"They approved the blood trials because we claimed

we could protect our own troops. If we could protect people within the strike zone, we could eliminate the enemy without fear of harming our own."

"And did you?" Alec interrupted. "Did you find the right formula to make this happen? Were you even close when the fire went up? Before the outbreak?" He stumbled over his words, swaying from side to side as he watched his colleague.

"I was close. We made progress every year. It was only a few years after Caroline died that our trial subjects started having fewer negative effects from the electric pulse. But then again, they altered the machine in that timeframe too. The pulse isn't a quarter as strong as it once was. There's no way to know if my study is what's helping people stay protected, or if the machine being weaker is what's keeping people alive."

"What do you think will happen?" Alec asked. "If someone took over Oscillation, it means they want to use the machine. Whether they're going to use the machine to hit one of our enemies or to hit us internally is unknown."

"We don't know who took over the machine, or if they now hold all of Oscillation in their grips."

"What about Vic?" Alec asked, the idea coming to his mind quickly. He spoke before thinking it over and regretted the question as soon as he'd asked it. Gretchen's glare drove into his gaze and he faltered. "He told you not to get on the plane. Did he know this was coming?"

"According to the files Vic led me to, they were going to do tests today. I don't think he was involved in the takeover. I think they planned the takeover to coincide with the trials. Everyone would be so preoccupied; it'd be easy to get through security."

"What about the fire?" Alec asked. Again, without thinking of his words.

Gretchen shook her head.

Alec could see her patience running thin, a common occurrence when he started getting too tipsy. She took another sip from her glass of whiskey and looked around. He could tell her nerves had settled since first learning someone took over the machine. Now it was a waiting game for when, or if, a strike would hit. Alec couldn't help but wonder if they'd fall from the sky, the plane's electrical circuits fried and the pilot unable to fly the aircraft.

"I don't think the fire was an accident," Gretchen whispered.

Alec turned to her. "I think there was a breach," Alec confessed.

"You do?" Gretchen asked.

"The outbreak. How could it sprint through your test subjects, but not the general community? How was it pinpointed for your patients? You cleared it up and then a fire comes out of nowhere?"

"People think my trials caused the outbreak, and that's why it didn't spread to anyone else."

"They can't prove it." Alex shook his head. "The trials didn't cause that outbreak. You isolated it and stopped it from spreading. How you did that, I don't know. But if it was a true outbreak, it wouldn't have only taken down a few, it would have taken down the entire population."

"A breach then." Gretchen sighed. "How would someone get into the compound? Your force-field is impregnable."

"I don't think they broke in," Alec said, nervous to voice his theory. He took a deep breath. "I think the breach came from within. Someone in Oscillation, someone from our team, did this. And I think it's the same person who just gained control of the machine."

THE FALL

CHAPTER 8

The first clue the pulse had hit the airplane was the jolt. The plane bumped and alarm sirens sang out. Gretchen could see confusion and fear gripping the surrounding people. The whiskey had already settled into her bloodstream, calming her.

The second sign was the excruciating pain that bolted through her mind, vibrating and shocking her. Her thoughts bubbled, and the pulse burned behind her eyes.

The flight attendant staggered to the communication hub at the front of the plane and picked up the phone to speak to the pilot. Her long ponytail swung uncontrollably. Gretchen saw a spark fly from the phone to the flight attendant's hand. She screamed and dropped the phone, stumbling to the wall for balance. The lights flickered throughout the cabin.

Then, complete silence.

Silence, then an insistent buzzing.

Gretchen heard air whistling as she looked out the window. She saw the engines spark. Flames took hold.

The entire engine blew apart, pushing the plane sharply to the right.

Screams filled the cabin as the flight attendant fell to the ground. She pulled herself up and took hold of the nearest empty seat, looking at her fellow flight attendants. No one knew what to do.

Gretchen leaned toward Alec and reached for his hand. His hand grasped hers. She gripped the armrest with her other hand, her knuckles turning white.

Air masks fell from the ceiling. Alec pulled his hand from Gretchen's, and she watched him place his mask on himself. She followed his lead and pulled the second hanging mask to her face. The elastic band snapped her cheek as she pulled it into place. The sting further heightened her senses.

Alec grabbed her hand once more.

"Put your heads down! Everyone, put your heads between your knees!" The flight attendant screamed the order to the passengers, though half of them could not hear her. A cacophony of noise overwhelmed all senses. Terror moved everything in slow motion, fear on every face.

Gretchen squeezed Alec's hand and glanced out the window. She saw sparks from the engine, black smoke streaking from the wing. Past the wreckage, the desert came into view. The horizon slanted, coming closer and closer.

Alec's hand pulled from hers. He clutched his phone, turning it toward her. After reading the screen, Gretchen locked eyes with him. They already knew what the text tried to warn. It was over for them.

I'm sorry. It's already hit the northwest.
It's coming your way. I wasn't fast enough.

In those last few moments, amid the screaming and crying passengers, Gretchen felt a wave of calm surround her. Security encased her. Instead of her life flashing before her eyes, she thought of Oscillation and who had taken it over, who decided the fate of Alec and herself. Whoever it was, they decided the fate of the nation long before this moment. The unknown of tomorrow was a fleeting thought, no longer under her control, no longer her problem to worry about.

She had a part in this, the destruction and terror. Working for the Director, the man who built this empire, meant she was as much to blame as anyone else. Alec, the clumsy secretary in the corporate office, the friend of Alec's who warned them of their fate. All to blame, but also innocent. Though they had minor connections to the imminent destruction, they all chose to work for the company. They knew the gravity of what the company could do, of what the machine would do. Now, a different type of gravity pulled the plane down.

The whiskey dulled her mind, but she truly *felt* for the

first time in years. She felt pain, anger, sadness, and complete understanding. She was grateful for the dizziness as she squeezed Alec's hand once more and closed her eyes.

Continue the series with

Book one of The Shockwave:

TRANSIENT PULSE

BOOK 1 OF THE SHOCKWAVE SERIES

TRANSIENT PULSE

LAURA JUNTUNEN

ABOUT THE AUTHOR

Laura Juntunen is a reader, writer, and podcaster. When not working or writing, Laura enjoys physical activities, motorcycling, spending time with family and friends, and diving into dystopian and fantasy novels with a glass of whiskey in her hand. She reads, writes, and podcasts out of southern Indiana, where she lives with her partner, Brian and their two bunnies, Flop and Buck.

KEEP IN TOUCH

IG: **@LauraJayLive**
www.LauraJayLive.com
Laura@LauraJayLive.com

ALSO BY LAURA JUNTUNEN

THE SHOCKWAVE SERIES
  The Fall
  Transient Pulse
  Oscillation Rising
  Static Equilibrium

www.ingramcontent.com/pod-product-compliance
Lightning Source LLC
Chambersburg PA
CBHW020600130626
46552CB00007B/2973